
Please return this book on or before the date shown above. To renew go to www.essex.gov.uk/libraries, ring 0345 603 7628 or go to any Essex library.

Essex County Council

Raintree is an imprint of Capstone Global Library Limited, a company
incorporated in England and Wales having its registered office at 7
Pilgrim Street, London, EC4V 6LB – Registered company number: 6695582

www.raintree.co.uk
myorders@raintree.co.uk

Text © Capstone Global Library Limited 2016
The moral rights of the proprietor have been asserted.

Designed by Hilary Wacholz
Original illustrations © Capstone 2016
Illustrated by Bradford Kendall
ISBN 978 1 4747 1056 5 (paperback)
20 19 18 17 16
10 9 8 7 6 5 4 3 2 1

British Library Cataloguing in Publication Data
A full catalogue record for this book is available from
the British Library.

Printed and bound in China.

These are the last days of the Library of Doom.

The forces of villainy are freeing the Library's most dangerous books. Only one thing can stop Evil from penning history's final chapter — the League of Librarians, a mysterious collection of heroes who only appear when the Library faces its greatest threat.

Deep down in the Black Shelves,
no one can hear you scream.

CONTENTS

Chapter 1

CLIFF HANGERS

"Face it," Lorenzo says. "You can't find that book!"

"I can find any **book**," Slate says.

"Just don't drop the book on me!" Breeze says.

The three young workers are Pages. They live and work in the Library of Doom.

The friends are special Pages. They are called Cliff hangers.

They travel up and down the tallest shelves on **STEEL** wires.

These **STEEP** shelves are called the Cliff of Notes.

The Pages hang **hundreds** of metres in the air. They work late at night.

"No one has found that book in years," says Lorenzo.

Slate grins. "That's because nobody has asked me," he says. "I could be a librarian if I wanted to."

Zing!

Breeze swings next to Lorenzo.

"What's the book called?" she asks.

Before he speaks, Lorenzo looks to his left. Then he looks to his right. "It's called SCRAWLER," he whispers.

Slate stares at Lorenzo.

He doesn't say a word.

He knows **WHERE** the book is.

Chapter 2

THE DARE

"Why is that book special?" Breeze asks.

"Because it's not just a book," Lorenzo says. "It's a **trap**. And none of the librarians can find it."

Breeze narrows her eyes.

"Are you okay, Slate?" she asks. "You don't look too good."

Slate **frowns**. Lorenzo laughs.

"He's just worried that he won't find the book," Lorenzo says. "I **DARE** you to find it."

Lorenzo smirks. "If you find it, I'll do your work for a week," he says.

Slate takes a deep breath. "Deal!" he shouts.

Swiftly, he swings away.

Chapter 3

THE BLACK SHELVES

Slate knows where to look. But he needs to keep it a **secret**.

He saw the book weeks ago.

He was exploring the **BLACK** Shelves.

Slate can't tell anyone how he found the book. He had a torch with him when he was exploring.

Light is **forbidden** in the Black Shelves.

Soon, Slate stands at the entrance to the Shelves.

He steps inside. He can't hear his footsteps.

There is no sound inside the Black Shelves.

He takes a few more steps. He pulls out his torch.

Slate sneaks down the paths between the Black Shelves. Every shelf is packed with books.

Every time he passes a shelf, dark books slide out **TOWARDS** him.

They want Slate to open them.

The boy ignores. He keeps walking.

The **angry** books squirm back into their shelves.

Slate finally reaches the shelf he seeks.

The shelf holds only **ONE** book.

The other books are afraid of it, he thinks.

The beam from Slate's torch touches the book.

Slate reads the title:

SCRAWLER

He has won Lorenzo's dare.

Chapter 4

SCRAWLER

The book **burns** the boy's hand.

"Ah!" he yells.

Slate grabs his hurt hand. He **DROPS** the book and the torch.

Laughter **echoes** through the darkness.

"I knew you'd be back," someone says.

Slate rubs his burnt hand. He can't see who is speaking.

He wants to run away. Instead, he walks back towards the entrance. I am **not** a coward, Slate tells himself.

"You," someone growls. "You may leave the Black Shelves now." "Your light and your scream were all I needed."

Slate stumbles through the **darkness**. His hands guide him back to the entrance.

He realizes he is outside again. He can hear his footsteps.

But he still can't see anything. Slate reaches for his face.

He has no eyes.

The Scrawler has **DEFACED** him.

Chapter 5

THE PAGE TURNS

Slate hears the **EVIL** laughter. It is right next to him.

"Now you know the secret," Scrawler says. "The reason the Librarians **trapped** me in that book."

Slate hears the creature throw a book onto the floor.

"But it's too late," the Scrawler cries. "I'm going to deface all of their pages!"

Slate feels a breeze. Now the Scrawler's **laughter** is far away.

Slate hears shouts and **SCREAMS**, too.
The Pages are being defaced one by one. He
has to warn Lorenzo and Breeze.

Slate hears a new sound. Boots scrape on
the stone floor.

"I don't get many visitors to the Black
Shelves," says someone.

Slate knows that voice. It belongs to the Blue Librarian. The one who cannot see. Slate feels an open book shoved into his hands. "Hold on!" says the Librarian.

"What is this?" Slate asks.

"You released the Scrawler," says the Blue Librarian. "Only YOU can stop him now."

"How?" Slate asks.

"This will close the book on the Scrawler," the Blue Librarian says. "And perhaps on me."

"What do you mean?" asks Slate.

A **BLAST** of hot, fiery wind buffets the boy's body.

"Ahhhhhhhhh!" The Blue Librarian cries.

The wind suddenly stops. The fire is gone.

The book in Slate's hand is closed.

The boy still cannot see. But he can feel the Scrawler **moving** under the book's cover.

"Return the book," the Librarian says. His voice comes from far away. "Return it for me..."

"But I can't see!" Slate says.

"You will," The Blue Librarian says. His voice is just a **whisper**.

Slate slowly steps back inside the doorway.

Whoosh!

This time he feels a cold, **icy** wind.

A uniform of stiff leather now covers his body. Slate cannot see it, but he knows the leather is blue.

He has become a **LIBRARIAN**.

GLOSSARY

buffets hits something with great force many times

deface ruin the surface of something, usually with writing or drawings

diamond very hard, usually colourless stone that is a form of carbon and is often used in expensive jewellry

forbidden not permitted or allowed

ignores does nothing in response to something or someone

page one side of a sheet of paper in an open book. Also, a page is a young boy or girl who works as a servant or assistant for an important person.

scrawl write or draw something very quickly or carelessly

steep very high, or rising or falling very sharply

DISCUSSION QUESTIONS

1. Slate and the other pages work while hanging hundreds of metres in the air. Can you think of anyone else who works like this? Would you want to do their jobs?

2. What do you think happened to the Blue Librarian? Why?

3. Find the very first word used in the story. Why do you think the author chose that word? What does it have to do with the book's plot?

WRITING PROMPTS

1. Imagine you are one of Slate's friends. You work in the Library of Doom with him. What would your job be? Write down a list of what you would do there every day.

2. Slate is good at finding books because he explores a lot by himself. Where do you think he will go next? Write a short story about his next adventure.

3. Slate has become the new Blue Librarian. What kinds of powers does he now have? Write a short paragraph about his new abilities.

THE AUTHOR

Michael Dahl is the prolific author of the bestselling *Goodnight, Baseball* picture book and more than 200 other books for children and young adults. He has won the AEP Distinguished Achievement Award three times for his non-fiction, a Teachers' Choice Award from *Learning* magazine, and a Seal of Excellence from the Creative Child Awards. He is also the author of the Hocus Pocus Hotel mystery series and the Dragonblood books. Dahl currently lives in Minnesota, USA.

THE ILLUSTRATOR

Bradford Kendall has enjoyed drawing for as long as he can remember. As a boy, he loved to read comic books and watch old monster films. He graduated from the Rhode Island School of Design with a BFA in Illustration. He has owned his own commercial art business since 1983. Bradford lives in Rhode Island, USA, with his wife, Leigh, and their two children, Lily and Stephen.